Little Miss Miss

Jeff Gottesfeld

SADDLEBACK
EDUCATIONAL PUBLISHING

red rhino books™

Body Switch	The Hero of	Sky Watchers
Clan Castles	Crow's Crossing	Standing by Emma
The Code	I Am Underdog	Starstruck
Fish Boy	Killer Flood	Stolen Treasure
Flyer	**Little Miss Miss**	The Soldier
Fight School	The Lost House	Too Many Dogs
The Garden Troll	The Love Mints	Zombies!
Ghost Mountain	Out of Gas	Zuze and the Star
The Gift	Racer	

With more titles on the way …

SADDLEBACK
EDUCATIONAL PUBLISHING
www.sdlback.com

ISBN-13: 978-1-62250-952-2
ISBN-10: 1-62250-952-8
eBook: 978-1-63078-175-0

Printed in Guangzhou, China
NOR/0215/CA21500098

19 18 17 16 15   1 2 3 4 5

Jordi ♥

Age: 12 (looks 25)

Special Skill: can spot an uneven spray tan from six blocks away

Best Sport: shopping

Future Goal: to be a TV spokesmodel

Best Quality: does what her mother says

Tracy

Age: 12 (looks 13)

Favorite Dinner: pork chops, green bean casserole, and ice-cold applesauce

Secret Wish: to spend a year in Spain

Future Goal: to be a high school PE teacher

Best Quality: is respectful of her parents

1
NEVER SAY NEVER

Tracy sighed as she walked into day camp. It was mid-June. School had ended two days before. She'd just finished sixth grade. She had been going to this camp every summer since she was seven years old. Her best bud Liza went there too.

After five years, the camp felt old. She knew the games. She knew the songs. She knew the staff. She knew how other kids went on big trips in the summer.

"I'll never go on a big trip," she said to herself. "We're too poor."

Tracy loved her parents. Her mom worked at a clinic. Her father helped people make gardens. They had good values. But they did not earn much money.

Liza was waiting for her by the handball wall. "Ready for summer?"

Tracy looked at Liza. She was small for her age. Her family had money. Her mom was a doctor. But they still sent Liza to day camp. The idea was to teach her that she was no better than anyone else. It had worked. Liza was the nicest person Tracy had ever met. Everyone liked Liza.

"Ready as I'll ever be," Tracy joked.

"There's a cool new girl on staff," Liza told her. "Her name is Ashley. She's doing waters sports. She was Miss All-State. But she isn't stuck-up. Not at all."

Tracy sniffed. Miss All-State was a big pageant. "How do you know it's true?"

"She told me."

"Maybe she's making it up."

Liza laughed. "Nah. I looked her up on my phone. Hey. There she is." She waved to a tall blonde girl in cutoffs and a camp T-shirt. "Yo, Ashley! Come meet Tracy!"

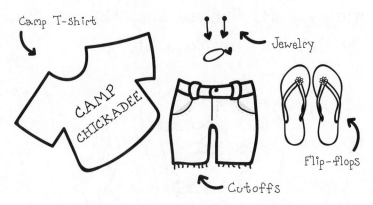

Camp T-shirt

CAMP CHICKADEE

Jewelry

Cutoffs

Flip-flops

Ashley trotted over. She was pretty, with a long neck and a warm smile. "Hey, Liza." She stuck her hand out to Tracy. "I'm Ashley. And you're …"

"Tracy. Tracy Jones."

Ashley shook her hand. "Liza said you guys come here every summer. I'll try to make it feel new."

"Is it true you won Miss All-State?" Tracy really wanted to know.

"That's a big y-e-s," Ashley said with a nod. "They pay for the winner's college. How come? You thinking about entering? I mean, in about five years."

Charge it to the All-State Pageant!

CREDIT CARD

Tracy shook her head. "It's not for me. Pageants are lame."

"Too bad. There's Little Miss Miss here

in two weeks. It's for twelve-year-olds. They want to find a cool girl role model. Okay prizes too. I was asked to judge it. But I don't have time."

"What kind of prizes?" Tracy asked.

"The winner goes to Washington, D.C., with her family. Something like that." Ashley's cell sounded with a text. She checked it. "Gotta run. See you at the pool. Nice to meet you, Tracy." Ashley trotted away.

Tracy had a bad cell phone. But Liza had a good one.

"Can I use your cell?" Tracy asked.

"Sure." Liza gave it to her. "Want to post a status?"

Tracy shook her head. She was starting to get an idea. "Nope. I want to look up this Little Miss Miss thing."

"What?!" Liza's jaw opened wide. "You're not a pageant girl. You'd never do that."

Tracy turned to her friend. "Liza, my bestie? Never say never."

2
BRICK WALL

"No way!" Tracy's mom was upset. "You cannot enter that ... that thing!"

Tracy had expected her mom to be a brick wall. So she stayed calm. "Little Miss Miss is not what you think. It's not about looks. It's about finding a great role model. It's fine. And wait until you meet Ashley."

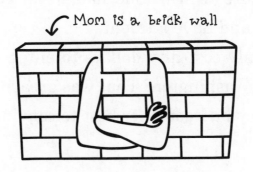

Mom is a brick wall

"Who's Ashley?" her dad asked.

"This girl at camp who gave her the idea," Mrs. Jones declared. She poured herself a little water. "Simon, I can't back this. Pageants stand for every value I hate."

Tracy had come home in a good mood. Camp had been fun. Ashley was a great swim teacher. There were new girls in her group who were good at sports. Liza was happy because of the new camp art center.

The best part of the day had been learning more about Little Miss Miss. Tracy looked it up. A girl had to be more than cute to win. She had to be good at sports and have a talent.

It only cost fifty dollars to enter. And a trip to Washington? That was great!

Tracy had done her best to convince her

mom and dad. She had eaten all her veggies. She washed the dishes. She'd even given a little speech.

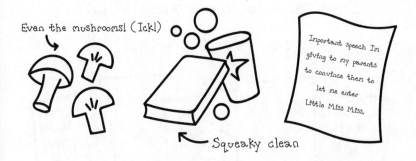

Even the mushrooms! (Ick!)

Important speech I'm giving to my parents to convince them to let me enter Little Miss Miss.

Squeaky clean

"This is how I grow up, Mom. Become a woman. Live my own life."

"Become a woman?" Her mother laughed. "You're twelve!"

Tracy knew when to quit. "Okay," she said. "I'm going up to my room to read."

She went upstairs. A few minutes later there was a tap on her door.

"Come in."

Her dad stepped into her room.

"I'd like to talk to you," he said. He pointed to the bed. "Can I sit?"

"Sure." She closed her book. "What's up?"

My favorite books!

"I talked to your mom about the Little Miss Miss thing. If you want to do it, you can."

Tracy wanted to scream with joy. Then she wanted to text Liza.

Instead she said, "That's great, Dad."

He looked grim. "But there's the entry fee. Do you have it?"

Tracy shook her head. "No. I was hoping you and mom might lend—"

"You mom does not want to give you money for this. But I'll lend it. And any other money you need. Like for clothes. Or whatever. *Lend.* Not give. Lend. You need to make a plan to pay it back."

Tracy threw her arms around her father. "Thanks, Dad. You're the best."

Her father grinned. "You'll never know what it took. Good luck."

New gardening boots

What *did* it take?

When her dad left the room, Tracy texted Liza. "Little Miss Miss! I'm in!!!"

Liza texted her right back. "I won't let u do this alone."

"OMG. You're entering?"

"I'm in! Let's be winner and runner-up!"

Tracy shouted with joy. By text, at least. "YESSS!!!"

3
COACH

Tracy and Liza were now part of Little Miss Miss. This was their first pageant. They needed someone to show them how to do it. Liza's mom was a busy doctor. Tracy's mom was *not* interested. Someone else would have to help them.

They went to camp early the next day. Ashley was swimming laps. They waited until she was done.

"Can we talk to you?" Tracy asked.

"Sure! Give me that towel," Ashley told them. She took off her swim cap. Her blonde hair fell loose. "What's up?"

Tracy got her the towel. "The Little Miss Miss thing? We both signed up."

Ashley grinned. Then she toweled off. "Really? That's great. You'll have fun."

Liza shook her head. "Not if we're newbies. We don't know what to do."

"It's our first pageant," Tracy added.

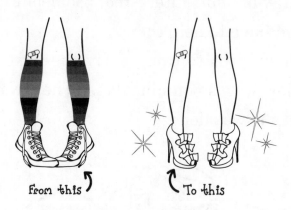

From this ❯ ❮ To this

"Good point," Ashley agreed. "There's a

16

lot to learn. How to walk. How to talk. How to act with the other kids. The judges see it all. They take notes. You always have to be on. Come on. Walk with me."

The three of them crossed the camp. Tracy was glad for the walk. It gave her a chance to think. She got a wild idea. "You should coach us," she told Ashley.

Ashley stopped. She turned to them and grinned. "Maybe. But you can't afford me."

Pageant Stars by
Ashley
• • • • • • $100 an hour

Tracy felt sick. She hadn't thought about money. "How much would you charge?"

Ashley seemed to think. It took a long time for her to speak. "Oh ... how about nothing?"

"Nothing?" Liza asked. "As in zero?"

"Nothing, as in zero. I need an idea for a summer essay for college. If I coach you, that could be it. I'll write about you guys." She wagged a finger at them. "I'm not easy. If we're in it, we're in it to win it. Are we in it to win it?"

Ashley offered the girls fist bumps. One with each hand. Tracy bumped her right fist. Liza bumped the left one. The deal was made.

4
THE LOVELY JORDI

The girls worked hard with Ashley. She was tough. But caring.

Training!

The first pageant meeting was ten days later. It was in the high school gym.

Tracy asked her mom to come. She said no. "You may do this," she told Tracy. "But I will not be part of it."

That was hard for Tracy to hear.

At least when her mom met Ashley, she liked her. But she was still not going to be part of it. Tracy went to the meeting with Ashley and Liza.

The woman in charge was old. She spoke slowly. "I'm Mrs. Cole. Welcome, welcome! We are so glad you are here! It is going to be so fun!"

Judges' Table

Mrs. Cole had the three judges wave to the crowd. Then she gave out some info. The first event would be that same day, at the town rec center. There would be events each day until Saturday night. That night would be the finals. For the top ten girls.

The meeting ended. Everyone clapped again. There was a pretty blonde girl at the end of Tracy's row. She was with her mom. They wore matching outfits: white shorts and white shirts. They had the same fake smile. Same fake clap. And the same mean eyes.

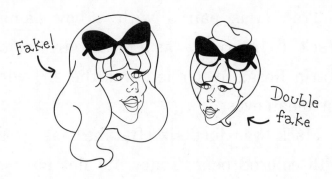

Fake!

Double fake

Tracy did not even know the girl's name. But right away she felt the girl would be trouble.

The first event was about art. Each girl was teamed with a little kid. Each team got a white hat. There were pens on the table. The idea was to make the hats look cool.

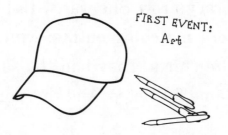

FIRST EVENT:
Art

Tracy was paired with a boy named Mack. To her right was a pretty girl named Maria Rosa. To her left was the girl with the mean eyes.

Mack was just six. But he was great with colored pens. Tracy did not have to do much. Mack was so good that Tracy left him for a moment. She decided to meet the girl with the mean eyes. Maybe she was actually nice.

"Hi," she said. She put out her hand to the girl. "I'm Tracy."

"I'm Jordi Mann," the girl said. "Now go away."

Tracy was stunned. "What did you say?"

"I said, 'go away.' Now."

Whoa. Jordi Mann was as mean as she looked.

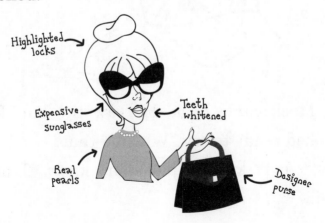

Highlighted locks

Expensive sunglasses

Teeth whitened

Real pearls

Designer purse

Tracy went back to Mack. He was done with the hat. It looked great. He wanted to get some water. Tracy said that was fine.

She went over to see how Maria was doing. Maria was working with a young girl. She said a warm hello. Then Tracy went back to her spot. She looked down at Mack's hat. There was now a huge spot of black ink on it. Right on top.

Mack came back. He saw the hat. He looked ready to cry. "Who did that?"

"I don't know. I just don't know," Tracy said.

Someone had messed up the hat. To mess *her* up. She scanned the room. Jordi met her eyes. The girl waved coldly. Then she tapped the top of her head. Like a hat was there.

Whoa. It had been Jordi. But Tracy had no proof. Without proof, she was stuck.

5
THIS ISN'T OVER

The next day after camp was Little Miss Miss sports. They did it at the rec center. There were all kinds of events. There was a soccer ball kick. A baseball throw. It ended with swimming races.

EVENT TWO:
Sports

Liza was not sporty. Ashley mostly

coached her. Jordi was also not very sporty. Her mother yelled at her a lot. Everyone heard it.

During a break, Liza came over to Tracy.

"How you doing?" Tracy asked.

"Bad. I stink at this stuff. Hey. Want to know what I know about Jordi?"

Tracy looked over at the blonde girl. Her mom was rubbing her legs. "She's a witch?"

"Nope. But she's not from here. She came from another state to do Little Miss Miss. Pageants are her life."

Jordi flew from here

Where everything's bigger: hair, egos, and pageants!

Dallas, Texas

"How do you know all that?"

Liza tapped her cell phone. "I read her blog. Her mom writes it."

"I told you about the hat thing. Watch your back," Tracy advised.

Ashley joined them. "I'll watch her too."

After that was Tracy's swim race. It would be a hundred meters. Jordi was next to her at the start. Liza was not in this race.

"Hi, Tracy!" said Jordi. She sounded friendly.

Tracy eyed Jordi. She did not trust her at all. "Hi."

"You're really good at sports," Jordi told her. She smiled.

"Thanks," Tracy said. It was odd. Jordi was being so nice.

"Hey!" Jordi shouted. "Tracy! Watch out! There's a big bee right by your neck!"

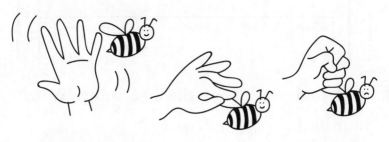

Tracy reached for the back of her head—
Toot!

A loud horn started the race. Tracy kept slapping at the bee. Everyone else dove into the pool. Then Tracy got it. There was no bee. Jordi had messed her up again. She dove into the water. But she was a good ten feet behind all the other girls.

She swam with all she had. Halfway into the last lap, she was even with Jordi.

"Go, Tracy!" Liza yelled.

"Come on, Tracy. Come on!" Ashley shouted.

No way would she let Jordi beat her. She kicked harder. When she touched the pool wall, a judge was there. So were Ashley and Liza.

"The winner!" the judge shouted. "Tracy's the winner!"

"Way to go!" Ashley cheered.

Tracy was happy she won. Maria came in second. Jordi was third.

"This isn't over," Jordi told her.

Tracy got out of the pool. Then she looked down at Jordi. "Today it is. And, Jordi? Watch out for bees."

6
LOSER

The next day was the cooking contest. It was like the TV show *Chopped*. A big kitchen was set up in the high school gym. There were dozens of stoves. Each girl got the same box of food. They had one hour to cook something great.

Ashley had worked with the girls on

their cooking. They had made many meals. Liza was good at cooking. Tracy wasn't so good. She hoped she could make something decent.

Tracy wanted to talk to her mom before she left. Almost all the other moms came to every event. But not Tracy's mom. Tracy wondered if the judges might hate that. Most of all, it made Tracy feel lonely.

Her mom was behind the house. Tracy saw her watering the garden.

"Hey, Mom?"
"Yes, sweetie?"

"I wanted to know …" Tracy was not sure how to say it. "I guess … I wonder if you would come with me today. It would make me feel good."

Her mom sprayed water on some beans. "I bet it would make you feel good. But it wouldn't make me feel good. You know what I think of pageants."

Tracy felt a lump in her throat. "I hoped maybe you'd changed your mind."

Mrs. Jones softened. "I know this is hard for you. Be strong. Okay?"

Tracy wasn't sure how strong she could be. Then a car horn tooted twice. "Well. That's Ashley. I've got to go."

"You're in good hands with her. See you later."

Tracy headed for Ashley's car. She was

still sad. Her mom didn't even wish her good luck.

"Two minutes!" Mrs. Cole called from the stage.

Tracy stirred what was in the pan. It was all veggies. That's what had been in her box. Also, some potato chips. She didn't use the chips. She put the veggies into a stir-fry. She added lots of salt. It smelled good. She hoped the judges would like it.

They didn't.

Onion   Zucchini   Peas   Chips

"Ugh!" said the man who came to taste her food. "Sorry, Tracy. This won't do. It tastes like a salt mine."

This was bad news. But worse news was Jordi. The judges loved her dish. It was a veggie dip. She used the chips to serve it.

The judges rated the dishes. Jordi was first. The nice girl Maria was second. Liza had made a stew. She was in the middle. Tracy was last.

Jordi's winning dish

She shook her head. It would be hard for her to win now. Very hard.

She was about to leave. Jordi and her mom walked up.

"Nice try, loser," Jordi's mother said.

"Thanks," Tracy told her. "I'm sure glad you're not *my* mom."

7
SHARK MOM

A few moments later, Tracy felt bad. Jordi had an awful mom. What if she and Liza could help Jordi? It might change her life.

Smiley & fake on the outside

Awful & ugly on the inside

She talked it over with Ashley and Liza.

They agreed it was worth it. They would try one more time to make friends with Jordi. Liza said she would do most of the talking. Tracy was glad. Everyone liked Liza.

She spotted Jordi and her mom about to leave.

"Let's do it," she told Liza. "Right now."

They walked over to them.

"Jordi? Can we talk to you?" Liza asked. "Alone?"

Jordi's mother stepped between the girls and Jordi. "What for?"

"Oh, you know, Mrs. Mann. It's kid stuff," Liza said. "So, is it okay?"

"My Jordi doesn't care about kid stuff. And she doesn't want to talk to you alone."

"Is that true?" Tracy asked Jordi. "Is that what *you* want?"

Jordi stood silent. She looked at Tracy. Tracy felt some hope. Maybe this was the time Jordi could be free. Then her mom cleared her throat. She gave Jordi a cold look. Jordi seemed to shake a little.

"Forget it," Jordi said. She could not look at the girls. "After the pageant, I'll never see you guys again. Never ever. Don't ask me to care about you. Don't talk to me again. But, hey. Have a nice life. Okay?"

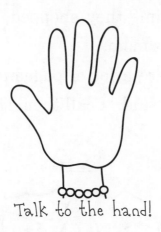

Talk to the hand!

Then her mother put a hand on her arm. "Come on, Jordi. We're out of here."

They walked away.

Two hours later, Tracy and Liza were at a thrift store. Each needed two outfits. One for the talent show the next day. The other was for Saturday night. Ashley helped them out. She had great taste. They spent very little money. They loved their outfits. But the whole time they shopped, they talked about Jordi's mom.

"There are a lot of pageant moms like her," Ashley said. "I call them sharks."

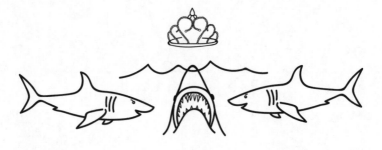

"Since they chew people up?" Tracy asked.

"Yup. And also, sharks have tiny brains," Ashley told them.

Tracy tried to think of Jordi's mom with a shark's body. It was a funny picture. "What do you do about them?"

Funny picture

Ashley shrugged. "Nothing. I just try to win. Doing well is the best way to get back at them."

Tracy nodded. The main thing was not to let Jordi and her mom get to her. It was easy to say. But it was hard to do.

8
TAPPED OUT

Friday was Little Miss Miss talent day. After her bad cooking, Tracy had to do well. She planned a magic act. She worked and worked at it.

The show was outdoors at the day camp.

There was a big stage. All the girls sat up there. Tracy and Liza were side by side. Campers and parents sat below. The judges were at a table. Mrs. Cole called each girl to perform for ninety seconds.

"And now," she said. "Please welcome Jordi Mann!"

Jordi came up. She wore a gold dress and a gold hat. She had a gold cane in her hands.

Jordi's talent outfit

"Look at her mom." Tracy pointed to Jordi's mom. She wore the same outfit as Jordi. Same hat. Even the same gold cane.

Liza shook her head. "That's so lame."

"I still feel bad for her," Tracy said.

Jordi's talent was tap dancing. Music played. Jordi's feet flew. Her tapping was great. Good enough to be a pro. She used the cane in her dance. Her dance ended. Jordi bowed. The crowd went wild. Even the judges clapped.

Tracy was stunned at how good she was. She knew that Jordi had just made the finals.

Other girls got called. Some girls played music. Maria sang. Liza told jokes. Tracy waited and waited. Finally, Mrs. Cole called her name. "Let's welcome Tracy Jones!"

There were a few claps. She looked out at the crowd. So many kids. Some many parents. But not her own. She saw Jordi's mom staring. There was hate in her eyes.

After that, she saw Ashley. Her coach gave two thumbs-up.

"I can do this," Tracy said to herself.

Tracy asked a young girl to come out of the crowd to help her.

"What's your name?" she asked the little girl.

"I'm Kori."

Tracy grinned. "Well, Kori? Did you know you have money behind your ear?"

Tracy reached back there. Then she opened her hand. Inside was a quarter. And then a silver dollar. And then a dollar bill. Kori laughed happily.

↑ You're rich!

"You're rich, Kori! Keep the money. Now go back to your seat. Big hand for Kori!"

The crowd clapped a little louder. Next came some card tricks. The crowd liked them. But Tracy's magic was not as good as Jordi's dancing. She knew it too. She got less clapping than Jordi.

Is this your card?

It took a minute for Mrs. Cole to name the winners. Jordi was at the top of the list. Tracy and Liza were in the middle. Tracy didn't think she would make the finals. Jordi in? Tracy out? She couldn't even think about it.

9
WIPEOUT

Saturday night. The Little Miss Miss finals.

Ashley had told the girls the finals were big. Tracy was shocked by *how* big. The hotel ballroom looked like a movie set. There was even a spotlight outside. A runway went down the center of the room. The huge crowd sat at long tables. They ate good food. Some people had to stand.

Tracy had asked her parents to come. Again, her mom held firm.

"I think you will learn more from me not being there."

Tracy thought about the last week. All the work she'd done. How lonely she felt. She didn't yell at her mom. But she did talk about her feelings. "I just feel bad. And I'd feel better if you were there."

"I can't come. Not if I don't agree with it."

Tracy blinked away some tears. There were so many things she wanted to say. How this was not about her mother. How it was about Tracy. How much she learned from Little Miss Miss. She learned to put up with a girl she did not like. She learned to do things even if she was not good at them.

Let's not forget this disaster!

She could have been mad at her mom. She chose to be kind. "Okay, Mom. Thanks for letting me be in it."

The girls waited backstage to start. There would be an opening walk on the runway.

All the girls would be in it. Then Mrs. Cole would name the final ten.

Tracy wore a black dress. Liza had on a red skirt and sparkly black top. Maria came up to them. She looked great. "We haven't really talked much. I just wanted to say good luck, guys."

Liza's

Tracy's

Tracy smiled. "You too."

Maria nodded. "Maybe we can hang later in the summer."

"We'd like that," Liza told her. They all traded numbers.

Music began. Mrs. Cole spoke over the PA. "Let's say a big hello to our Little Miss Miss girls!"

The opening parade started. It went down the runway. The room got loud with cheers. Tracy was two girls behind Liza. She was three behind Jordi. Many girls had fans and family.

She saw a sign for Jordi: GO, JORDI!

And one for Maria: WE LOVE MARIA!

There were no signs for Tracy. It made

her feel bad all over again. She looked one more time for her parents.

That was when she tripped on a crack in the runway.

10

THE WINNER

Tracy almost fell. She was lucky she didn't. But everyone saw. She looked over at a judge. He wrote something down.

That was it. She was sure she was done. No way would they pick her now. She barely listened when the final ten were selected.

Mrs. Cole milked the moment. "I will call a name. Ten girls in all. Each girl will come to the edge of the stage."

She took a long time between names. Jordi was named fourth. Her mom screamed like she was at a rock show. Girl after girl was called.

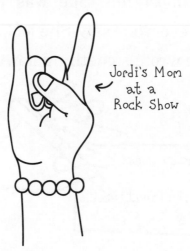

Jordi's Mom at a Rock Show

Oh well. Tracy spotted Ashley in the crowd. She looked sad.

"Number nine ... Maria Rosa!"

Maria joined the other finalists. She had a large group of fans. They cheered for her. Tracy was glad. Maria was a great girl.

One more name left to go.

Drumroll please ...

Mrs. Cole turned to the girls. "Last name. Girls, exit the stage if it isn't yours. Sit with your families. Thank you for being part of Little Miss Miss." Then she faced the crowd again. "Our final finalist is ... Tracy Jones!"

Tracy was amazed. They had picked her. Liza, Maria, and the other girls clapped.

Liza pumped her fists. "Go get 'em!"

Tracy hugged her bestie hard. "Thanks."

She moved to the front of the stage. She held hands with Maria. It was nuts. She was in. She saw Jordi glare at her. It felt good to smile back.

The ten girls got to do their talent again. People liked Tracy's magic, but they loved Jordi's dance.

Then came the last event of Little Miss Miss. Each girl took a question from the judges. She had thirty seconds to respond.

The question could be about anything. Sports. Music. The news. Anything at all. It was a test of how each girl did under pressure. After that part, the judges would vote for the winner.

Jordi was asked about the best book she had ever read.

THE
**BEST
BOOK**
EVER WRITTEN

By The Best Author

I thought Jordi just shopped

"I loved *The Cat in the Hat*," she said. "It gave me a love for reading. I have read all my life. My mom taught me when I was little. There are lots of books next to my bed."

Tracy thought that sounded like a total lie. There was no way to check. But it made the judges nod. Jordi looked smug. Tracy sighed. That would be hard to beat.

There were only two girls left to go. Maria answered a news question in both English and Spanish. The crowd loved that.

I believe in world peace!

¡Creo en la paz mundial!

Finally, it was Tracy's turn. She heard a little clapping near the doors. She peered into the room to see who it was.

No. It couldn't be. But it was.

Her mom and dad were there. They were

all dressed up. Her dad had a sign. Her mom had a sign. They held them up.

Wow.

"Tracy Jones?"

Tracy looked at the judges. The oldest one was waiting. "Yes?"

"Tracy? What about the last week has changed you?"

What? What a question! She'd hoped for one about sports. Or music.

She was quiet for a long time. She looked out at her mom. Her mother seemed to nod at her. Tracy told the truth.

"My mom and dad did not want me to enter. But they finally said okay. My friend and my coach helped me. I am stronger in my body. In my soul. In my mind. Most of all, in my heart. Little Miss Miss has helped me be a role model. Not just for other girls. But for myself. Oh yeah. My mom and dad are here now. Hi, Mom. Hi, Dad!"

Tracy waved to her folks. People cheered. She went back to the finalists. The cheering did not stop. She saw Jordi look at her. Was she dreaming, or was Jordi nodding with respect?

Music played for a few moments. Then Mrs. Cole came up to declare the winner.

"Thank you all for coming. As you can see, we have great girls. I am going to call up our top three. In third place, please welcome … Jordi Mann!"

Tracy glanced at Jordi. Jordi looked ready to cry. She plodded up to Mrs. Cole. The leader shook her hand.

Don't ruin your makeup, Jordi

Jordi's mother stood. "My girl was the best! Y'all robbed her!"

The crowd booed. Then it got quiet again.

"Now welcome our runner-up." Mrs. Cole looked at a card in her hand. "It's … Tracy Jones!"

No way! She was second. Not bad. Not bad at all.

The crowd cheered. Mrs. Cole placed a gold sash on her.

"And now our winner. Please welcome … Maria Rosa! Our new Little Miss Miss!"

Maria came forward. Everyone clapped. Maria got her crown. Tracy was the first to hug her.

"Thank you all for coming!" Mrs. Cole told the crowd.

Then Tracy was in a group hug too. Liza. Ashley. Her dad. And her mom. Little Miss Miss was over. Tracy had not won. But she still felt like a total winner.